Ginger's New Home

For anyone who has ever wanted a kitten – SM

STRIPES PUBLISHING
An imprint of Magi Publications
1 The Coda Centre, 189 Munster Road,
London SW6 6AW

A paperback original
First published in Great Britain in 2010

Text copyright © Sue Mongredien, 2010
Illustrations copyright © Emilia Robledo, 2010
Photographs copyright © iStockphoto.com, 2010

ISBN: 978-1-84715-118-6

A CIP catalogue record for this book is available
from the British Library.

Printed and bound in the UK.

10 9 8 7 6 5 4 3

Sue Mongredien
Illustrated by Emilia Robledo

Kitten Club

Ginger's New Home

stripes

Meet the Kitten Club girls!

Amy & Ginger

Mia & Smokey

Molly & Truffle

Ella
& Honey

Ruby
& Ziggy

Lily
& Buster

Chapter I

"Here we are!" said Mrs Wheeler, pointing through the car window. "Chestnut Farm. Oh, it's good to be here again, isn't it?"

Amy Wheeler wasn't so sure. She twirled a strand of her long blonde hair around her finger, and gazed out at the white-washed farmhouse surrounded by fields further down the track.

Chestnut Farm was where Aunty Sarah and Uncle Matthew lived. Amy's family didn't see them very often – although that was all set to change now, of course. Amy and her parents had lived in London until recently, but when Amy's mum had been offered a new job further north, they'd decided to move house, and, since yesterday, were living just down the road from Aunty Sarah. Amy's mum was thrilled to be near her sister, but Amy wasn't quite so excited. It wasn't that she didn't like her aunt and uncle, but she hadn't wanted to leave her old home and move so far from all her friends.

"Aunty Sarah told me you could start riding lessons here whenever you want to," her mum went on. "Some of the girls in the village ride at the farm, too. You're sure to make friends quickly."

Amy hoped her mum would be right. She'd been upset to say goodbye to her two best friends, Caitlin and Alice, and she was certain she'd never meet anyone as nice. How she wished her parents hadn't decided to leave London!

"And," her mum added, glancing back at Amy, "there's a surprise for you at the farm, too. Something that I think will really cheer you up."

"What sort of a surprise?" Amy asked.

Her mum smiled. "A cuddly kind of surprise," she replied.

Amy thought. "Has Aunty Sarah had a *baby*?" she asked.

"No," her mum said, laughing. "Although you could say the surprise was a sort of baby, I suppose…"

Amy frowned, not understanding. A sort of baby? A cuddly surprise? "A doll?" she asked, crossing her fingers that she was wrong. Now that she was eight, she felt too grown-up to play with dolls.

"Meow," her dad added helpfully from the driver's seat.

Meow? Amy felt a prickle of excitement. "Are we getting a *cat*?" she asked, hope rushing up inside her. "*Are we?*"

Amy hardly dared to believe it. She'd

wanted a cat for ages, but the road they'd
lived on before had been very busy, with
lots of cars and buses rushing by. Although
she'd pleaded with her parents a hundred
times, the answer had always been the same.
It wasn't a safe road for a cat.

Amy's dad parked the car and switched
off the engine, then turned round to Amy.
"Well, Aunty Sarah's cat Bess has had six
kittens," he said, smiling. "So…"

"Kittens?" Amy cried. Even better!
"We're getting a kitten!" she squealed, her
fingers fumbling to unclip her seat belt in
her eagerness to get out.

Her parents laughed. "Now that we're living on a nice quiet road, we thought a kitten might help you settle in to our new house," her mum replied. "Come on, let's go and have a peep at them."

Inside the big, warm farmhouse kitchen, Bess, the mother cat, was curled up in a box, watching over her kittens. Amy crouched down to look at them. Two cute tabby kittens were playing peepo with one another, whilst a mischievous-looking black kitten was practising pouncing on a scrap of newspaper. A smokey grey kitten was enthusiastically washing one of its back legs but as Amy watched, it lost its balance and toppled over with a surprised mew.

Another kitten, this one mostly white with tabby markings on its face and a stripey tail, was attacking the leg of a nearby stool, clinging on to it with tiny claws. The sixth kitten was pure ginger from nose to tail, and was snuggled up with Bess, fast asleep.

Amy watched them with delight. They were just so sweet with their little fluffy bodies, big round eyes and teeny paws! How was she ever going to pick only one? "Can I choose *all* of them?" she asked hopefully.

"Nice try." Her dad laughed. "But one is enough."

"They're adorable, aren't they?" Aunty Sarah said, putting a plate of biscuits on the table. "Take your time, Amy, there's no rush. Some other girls are coming round later to choose kittens too, but I've told them that you've got first pick."

Amy knelt down and watched the kittens. The tabby pair were now batting

each other with their paws, while the all-black kitten was rolling around with

the newspaper, tearing
and chewing it for all he
was worth. The grey kitten was
stalking an imaginary enemy, his
body low as he padded along.
The mostly-white kitten was
now fighting the bottom of the curtain by
the back door, and the ginger kitten was just
waking up. He stretched out his body …
and gave the cutest little sneeze!

"Bless you!" Amy giggled.

The ginger kitten blinked and shook out
his whiskers, and then gazed up at Amy, his
blue eyes round and curious. He gave a
friendly mew, as if saying hello, then got to
his feet and trotted over to her, rubbing his
head against her knee and rumbling with a
tiny purr.

Amy felt as if her heart was melting. "Hello there," she said, gently picking up the kitten and sitting him on her lap. His fur was the colour of pale apricots, with stripes of a deeper orange on his legs and tail. He had white whiskers and the cutest pink nose. He was so handsome!

Aunty Sarah smiled. "He's the friendliest kitten of them all," she told Amy.

Amy tickled the ginger kitten under his chin and he purred even louder, his whole body quivering. *The friendliest kitten of them all?* Right now, she could do with a new friend. "I'd like this one, please," she said, stroking the kitten's soft fur. "And I'll call him … Ginger."

"Perfect," Aunty Sarah said, crouching beside her and stroking the tiny kitten behind his ears. "Well, I hope you and Ginger are going to be very happy together."

Amy smiled as Ginger rolled on to his back so that she could stroke his fluffy tummy. "I think we will be," she said confidently. "We're going to be the best of friends, aren't we, Ginger?"

Prrrrrr, went Ginger, as if he was agreeing, and everybody laughed.

Chapter 2

Aunty Sarah made tea for Amy's mum and dad, and they sat around the table chatting. Amy stayed on the floor, with Ginger on her lap. The grey kitten trotted past her knee, and Ginger cheekily reached out to bat his tail, making him jump. Then, seeing Ginger, the grey kitten jumped on to Amy's lap too, and the two kittens began a rough-and-tumble play-fight. After a few moments, they both rolled off Amy and on to the floor, where they continued to tussle.

"Hey, hey!" Amy laughed. "No scrapping, you two."

The doorbell rang just then, and Aunty Sarah rose from her chair. "That might be Ella and Mia. They said they would pop in after their riding lesson."

Seconds later, Amy heard two excited voices from the hall. She stood up, suddenly feeling awkward and shy as two girls burst into the kitchen. The first girl had long auburn hair, which hung loose over her shoulders. She had green eyes like Amy, a wide smile and tons of freckles across her nose. "Ohhhh!" she squealed as she saw the kittens. "Look, Mia! Haven't they grown?"

The second girl, Mia, had black shoulder-length hair and brown eyes, and her ears were pierced with tiny silver studs. Both girls were wearing jodhpurs and T-shirts. They rushed over towards Bess and the kittens, hardly seeming to notice Amy's family.

"Girls, I'd like you to meet my niece, Amy," Aunty Sarah said. "She's just moved to the village and I'm hoping she'll start riding lessons with you two before long. Amy, this is Ella and Mia."

Ella smiled at Amy. "Hiya," she said. Then she looked at Aunty Sarah and grinned.

"I was on Jester today, Sarah. That pony is such a daredevil! He couldn't keep still for five minutes!"

Aunty Sarah's eyes twinkled. "Now, who does that remind me of?" she said. "Sounds like you and Jester are the perfect match. And how did you get on today, Mia?" She paused. "Mia?"

But Mia was too busy fussing over the kittens to answer. "Hello, Tiger, hello, Muffin!" she said to the tabby kittens, who were now playing tug-of-war with a piece of wool. "Hello, Marmalade," she said, tickling Ginger, who had scampered over to join them, his fluffy orange tail up in the air.

Amy stiffened. *Marmalade?* She wasn't sure she liked the thought of Mia having already named her kitten.

"Mia!" said Ella loudly. "Sarah's talking to you!" She winked at Amy. "Mia's away with the fairies half the time. Lives in a dreamworld!"

Mia spun round. "What was that?" Her eyebrows shot up as she saw that everyone was looking at her. "Sorry. Were you talking to me? I was just saying hello to Marmalade and the others."

"It's Ginger," Amy said quietly, the blood rushing to her face as Mia's gaze fell on her. "His name's Ginger."

Aunty Sarah came to Amy's rescue. "Yes, you'll have to stop calling him Marmalade now, Mia," she said. "Amy's going to have this kitten, and his new name is Ginger."

"Oh," said Mia. "Oops!" She grinned, and two dimples appeared in her cheeks. "Hello, I'm Mia," she said. "Sorry, I was so excited about seeing the kittens again, I didn't even notice you!"

"She's soooo rude," Ella teased. "Don't worry, we're not all like her around here."

Amy smiled shyly, and then let out a giggle
as the black kitten tried to scramble over one
of Ella's boots and went head over heels.
Meow! he said in surprise, shaking himself.

Everyone laughed. "Well, Ella and Mia,
you two get to choose your kittens next,"
Aunty Sarah said. "So who are your
favourites?"

Mia and Ella both knelt
down, their faces turning
thoughtful. Choosing a
kitten was serious stuff!

"I need a kitten who will
get on with Misty," Ella
said. "That's our other
cat at home," she
explained to Amy. She
scooped up the all-black cat,

who began fighting Ella's hand, kicking at it
with his back legs and trying to bite it.
"Maybe not you, Sooty," she laughed. "If
you did that to Misty, you wouldn't
be very popular!"

Mia, meanwhile, was
cuddling the grey kitten.
"I think you're the
cutest," she said, stroking
the kitten's head. "Sarah,
is it all right if I have
Smokey?"

"Of course it is,"
Aunty Sarah said. "As long as you're sure
your mum is keen on the idea now?"

"Yes, she's cool – thank goodness!"
Mia replied, then turned to Amy to explain.
"Mum said I couldn't have a kitten at first –

because I do so many after-school clubs and activities, she said I wouldn't have time to look after a pet as well. But I've promised to look after you really, really well, Smokey, don't worry!"

Amy smiled. "I'm glad she changed her mind," she said, kneeling down next to Mia and stroking Ginger.

"Ella, how about you, have you decided?" Aunty Sarah asked.

Ella was now cuddling the white kitten with the tabby face and tail, the one who'd been attacking the stool leg when Amy had first arrived. Now the kitten was purring away contentedly in Ella's arms as if she was the best behaved creature in the world!

"I'd like this one, please," Ella said. "You'd be nice to Misty, wouldn't you, Honey?"

"Wonderful," Aunty Sarah said. "That's three kittens gone in as many minutes. Your mums should be here to collect you soon, girls, so we can sort everything out then."

Just then, the doorbell went again. "That'll be them now, I should think," Aunty Sarah said. "Back in a tick."

But it wasn't Ella and Mia's mums at the door. Instead, three more girls appeared in the kitchen, followed by a brown-haired woman, who looked startled to see such a busy kitchen. "Oh gosh," she said. "Sorry, Sarah, I didn't realize you had company. Would you rather we came back later?"

"Not at all," Aunty Sarah replied. "The more the merrier. Everybody, this is Marie

Evans, one of our regular customers at the farm shop, and this is her daughter Molly, and…"

"And this is Lily, who lives down the road from us, and Ruby, Molly's best friend from school," Mrs Evans finished. "Word about the kittens has got around, thanks to my daughter!" Her eyes fell on Amy, Ella and Mia and she turned back to Aunty Sarah, suddenly anxious. "Ahh. Are there enough kittens left for everybody who wants one?"

"There's just enough," said Aunty Sarah.

"Girls, the ginger kitten, the grey kitten and the mostly-white kitten are taken, but the others all need a home, so take a look."

The new girls – Ruby, Lily and Molly – came over to where Amy, Ella and Mia were still kneeling with the kittens. Lily had short blonde hair and silvery-blue rectangular glasses, Ruby had funky braided hair and was dressed head to toe in pink, and Molly had wavy hair in a bob and wore a football shirt.

"Hi," said Ella. "I'm Ella, and this is Mia, and Amy. Amy's just moved to the village."

"Hi," chorused Molly, Lily and Ruby all at the same time – and everyone grinned. Soon all six girls were chatting away about the kittens, even Amy. Somehow having the kittens romping around doing funny things made her forget about feeling shy.

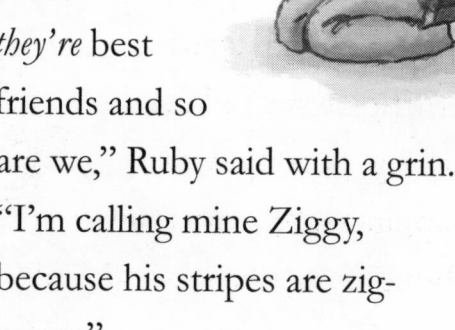

After a few minutes, Lily
chose the all-black kitten,
and christened him Buster,
and Ruby and Molly picked
a tabby kitten each.

"Because *they're* best
friends and so
are we," Ruby said with a grin.
"I'm calling mine Ziggy,
because his stripes are zig-
zaggy."

"And mine's called …
Truffle," Molly decided.
"Because she's just so sweet!"

"Wonderful," Aunty Sarah
said. "Well, I'm delighted that Bess's six
kittens are all going to such good homes.
The kittens need to stay with Bess for

another week, but you can come back and
collect them next
Saturday, OK?"

"Yay," cheered Molly,
who'd put Truffle on her
knee. She giggled as
Truffle began to knead
her leg, purring with
happiness. "I'm so excited
about having my own kitten!"

"Me too," Amy agreed. "I can't wait!"

Chapter 3

Over the next few days, Amy and her
family were busy unpacking and settling
into their new house. Luckily, it was the
summer holidays and school wasn't due to
start for another few weeks, so Amy had
plenty of time to arrange her new
bedroom. Her parents had painted it lilac,
and she decorated it with strings of fairy

lights, and lots of photos of her old friends.

Amy was trying her best not to think about going to a new school and having to make new friends. She was dreading not knowing anyone. What if nobody liked her? What if everyone already had best friends, and there was no place for her?

She distracted herself by planning for Ginger's arrival, and on Wednesday afternoon, she spent ages in the pet shop with her mum, choosing all the things he would need: special kitten food, food and water bowls, a litter tray, and a comfortable cat bed.

On the way home, she persuaded Mum to stop by at Aunty Sarah's, so that she could see Ginger again and show her aunt what they'd bought.

The six kittens were zipping around Aunty Sarah's kitchen, playing, chasing and clambering over their mother. It was only four days since Amy had seen them, but she was sure they'd grown already!

Ginger was playing with a little red ball that jingled as it rolled along. Amy bent down and picked him up, and Ginger immediately rubbed his head against her hand, rumbling with purrs. "Hello, Ginger," she said, feeling a rush of delight. "We've been buying lots of things for you. We're all ready for Saturday, when you'll come and live with us!"

"Did you get Ginger a brush?" Aunty

Sarah asked, pouring everyone tea. "Only I've got a spare one if not. With fluffy fur like Ginger's, it's important to keep him well-groomed."

"We didn't get a brush, no," Amy's mum said. "I hadn't thought about that. It's enough work getting Amy to brush her own hair, let alone a kitten's," she joked.

Amy took the small wooden brush Aunty Sarah was holding out and sat down with Ginger on her knee. "I'll brush Ginger's fur every day," she promised, running the soft bristles down his back. Ginger seemed to like being groomed and kept very still while she ran the brush over his fur.

"There," Amy said when she'd finished. "Now you're the smartest kitten in town!"

Aunty Sarah told Amy some other things about looking after kittens – that they needed lots of sleep, just like newborn babies, and how often and how much to feed them. Amy had stopped paying attention though because Ginger was attacking her trouser leg, leaping on her foot and tugging at the hem of her jeans like a mad thing. "Oh, Ginger," Amy giggled. "We're going to have such fun together, aren't we? I know it already."

At long last, it was Saturday again, and time to take Ginger home. Amy was dressed and ready to go by eight o'clock, but her mum insisted she had some breakfast first! By the time they arrived at Aunty Sarah's, Ruby, Lily and Molly were already there.

Amy suddenly felt shy again when she saw so many people, but she knew she had to be brave. Her mum began talking to the other grown-ups so she took a deep breath and went to join the girls. "Hi," she said, turning bright red as they all looked at her.

"Hi again," said Molly. She was wearing a different football shirt today, plus denim shorts and trainers. "It's Amy, right?"

Amy nodded. "Yes," she said, and then crouched down to pick up Ginger. "Hello there," she said, cuddling him.

Ruby was unhooking her kitten's tiny claws from where they'd got stuck in her pink T-shirt. "Hey, Ziggy!" she said. "Be careful. This is my favourite top!"

"Looks like Ziggy's attached to you already," Lily joked. "*Attached* to you – get it?" She smiled at Amy. "Are you looking forward to taking Ginger home?"

"Oh *yes*," Amy said. "I've wanted a cat for so long. I've been counting down the days!"

"Me too," Ruby said. "We haven't got a pet either – unless you count my little brother. He's a bit of an animal, only he isn't half as cute as a kitten!" She jumped as Ziggy made a lunge for her necklace and got his claws stuck in one of the beads. "Oh, Ziggy!" she laughed. "What are you like?"

The kitchen door opened again and in came Ella and Mia, both wearing riding clothes. "Hi, everyone," Mia said, her dimples flashing in her cheeks as she gave everyone a big smile. "It's Kitten Day!"

"Hi, guys," Ella said, raking a hand through her tousled hair. "Phew! That was a fab lesson, Sarah." She looked at Amy. "You *have* to come next time. We were doing jumps – it was so exciting!"

"Yes, have you made up your mind about lessons, Amy?" Aunty Sarah asked, overhearing.

Amy felt pleased that Ella had remembered. "I think I *would* like to give riding a go," she said. "But I've never ridden before – I don't think I'll be able to jump for a while!"

Ella grinned. "Maybe not," she agreed. "But we always have really good fun."

"And you'll be able to let us know how Ginger's getting on every week, too," Mia put in.

Lily folded her arms across her chest and pretended to pout. "Wah," she said, mimicking a baby noise. "Not fair. Everyone else is going to see each other again, except me."

The girls all laughed. Lily was a bit of a drama queen, Amy thought to herself with a smile.

"What are you on about? You'll see *me*," Molly reminded her. "I only live up the road!"

"I know but…" Lily gave a theatrical

sigh. "You two are always hanging out together," she said, gesturing towards Molly and Ruby. "And you three are going to have riding lessons together," she said, pointing at Amy, Ella and Mia. "And you'll all get to talk about the kittens without *me*!"

There was a moment's silence, and then Mia's face lit up as if she'd had an idea. "Well, maybe we should *all* meet up sometime. Hey, we could get the kittens together too, couldn't we?"

Aunty Sarah, who was making coffee, turned her head at Mia's words. "The kittens will have to stay indoors for another eight weeks, remember, until they've had their vaccinations," she put in.

"Oh," Lily said, looking disappointed. Then she smiled. "Still, *we* can all meet up

together, can't we? Us six girls. We could be like a club!"

"Yeah!" Ella said. "That's a wicked idea." She picked up Honey, her white and tabby kitten and cuddled her. "Hey! We could call ourselves Kitten Club!"

"Kitten Club! I love it." Molly laughed, stroking Truffle, who was winding around her legs like a fluffy ankle-warmer. "We could meet every week to see how the kittens are getting on."

"I'd like that too," Amy said, feeling less shy all of a sudden. "We could keep a sort of journal about our kittens."

"Yeah, and stick in photos of them!" Lily put in, her eyes shining.

"We could have code names too," Ruby suggested. "Secret code names that only

club members know about!"

Ella leaned forward eagerly. "What do you reckon, then?" she asked. "Are we all in?"

"Yes!" the others chorused at once, all grinning excitedly.

"Then that's settled," Lily declared. "Us six girls and our six gorgeous kittens are the official members of Kitten Club. Yay!"

Chapter 4

Amy felt much happier about having moved house as they took Ginger home later that morning. Not only had she got her very own kitten to look after and love, but she'd made five new friends and was now part of a club – Kitten Club!

The girls had agreed to meet the following Saturday afternoon at Lily's

house. "Don't forget to think of your secret code name," Lily reminded them as she gave out her phone number and address.

A secret code name… Hmmm. Amy hadn't had any bright ideas yet. As she was thinking, a meow came from the cardboard box that was next to her on the back seat, and a small ginger paw appeared through a tiny hole on one side. Poor Ginger! Aunty Sarah had put him in a box with a lid on so that he couldn't escape, but Amy was sure it must be scary, being in a dark box in a moving vehicle.

"Don't worry, Ginger, we'll be home soon," Amy soothed, stroking the little paw. "Nearly there."

Back home, Dad let them in, and Amy carried the box into the kitchen. Once the door was shut, she took the lid off the box and scooped up Ginger. She knelt down with him, stroking him and talking to him softly. She knew how scary it was to move house!

After a few minutes, Ginger jumped off her lap to explore. He trotted all around, sniffing everything. He had a drink from his new water bowl and ate some of the special kitten food they'd bought, then chased a piece of string Amy pulled around the room. But after a while, he began meowing and walking around the room as if he was looking for Bess.

Amy watched him anxiously. "He must be missing his mum, and his brothers and sisters. What if he doesn't want to live with us?"

Her mum put an arm around her. "He'll be fine," she said. "He's bound to miss them at first. We'll just have to give him lots of cuddles whenever he feels lonely, to make him feel at home. He'll soon settle in."

"He'll be the happiest kitten around, you'll see," Dad agreed.

Amy bit her lip, hoping they were right. She gathered Ginger up in her arms and pressed her face against his fur. "Don't worry, Ginger, I'm looking after you now."

That night, Amy carried Ginger's cat bed up to her bedroom so that he wouldn't be all alone. After her parents had said goodnight, she lay in the darkness, smiling as she heard Ginger moving around in his little cat bed.

She couldn't resist switching on her bedside lamp. "What *are* you up to?" she giggled. "Chasing your tail? Oh, Ginger!"

At the sound of her voice, Ginger gave a mew and climbed out of his bed. He scampered over towards Amy and she reached down to stroke him. He meowed again, louder this time. "Are you lonely?" Amy wondered. "Do you want to come up here and sleep with me?"

Ginger purred, as if that was *exactly* what he wanted! Amy scooped him up and put him on the duvet next to her, and Ginger purred and purred, his body vibrating like a little engine. Then he curled up, shut his eyes and went to sleep.

Amy hardly dared breathe in case she woke him. It was lovely to have a kitten

right there on her bed! But how was she
ever going to get to sleep? She didn't want
to disturb him by moving, and she was
worried she might roll on top of him in her
sleep. He was so tiny, she might squash him!

There was only one thing for it. Amy
inched away from him as slowly and
carefully as she could, then picked up her
pillow, turned off the lamp, and went to
sleep on the floor – leaving Ginger with the
bed all to himself!

Chapter 5

The next morning Amy woke up in her bed
… but Ginger was nowhere to be seen. She
rubbed her eyes in alarm, and stared all
around the room. She hadn't just *dreamed*
she'd got a new kitten, had she?

She pulled on her dressing gown and flew
downstairs. To her great relief, Ginger was in
the kitchen, pouncing on her dad's bare feet

as he made a cup of tea. "There you are!" she said, rushing over to her kitten. She cuddled him close and he patted her face with one of his paws. "Dad, I thought Ginger was going to sleep in my room?" she said.

"He was," her dad replied. "Until your mum and I looked in on you last night to see you sleeping on the floor – and Ginger in your bed!"

Amy stroked Ginger. "He was lonely," she explained.

"Hmmm," her dad said. "Well, we've decided that Ginger might be better off down here, near his litter tray and water bowl anyway. And that way, *you* get to sleep in your bed, not His Fluffy Highness!"

A few days passed, and Amy felt as if she had a new best friend in Ginger. She spent all her time with him. Her mum had started her new job now, while her dad was working in his office at home, but Amy was quite happy hanging out, just her and Ginger.

Amy's parents kept encouraging her to get out and about – to play in the garden, or join the local dance classes and riding school, but all Amy wanted to do was look after Ginger. She fed him every time he went to his food bowl. She played with him and brushed his fur. And whenever he seemed to be missing Bess, she'd give him a little treat. There was some whipped cream left over from pudding on Sunday, so she gave him a blob of that. There was some cold chicken in the fridge, so she slipped him a few pieces when her parents weren't looking. And one evening, when he seemed sad, she poured him a big saucer of lovely, creamy milk.

"There," she said, as he lapped it up greedily. "Is that yummy? Yes!" she said. "And am I the best kitten-mummy in the world? Yes!"

The next morning – Thursday – Ginger
seemed a bit off-colour. He'd been sick on
the kitchen floor and didn't want any
breakfast. Amy's mum had already left for
work, so Amy ran to fetch her dad. "Do
you think we should call the vet?" she asked
anxiously, watching as Ginger curled up in
bed and closed his eyes.

Her dad shook his head. "He'll be all
right," he said. "Kittens can be a bit sickly,
I suppose, just like babies are more prone
to being poorly than grown-ups. If he's sick
again, we can think about phoning the vet,
but I'm sure he'll be fine." Then he looked
at Amy. "I think *you* could do with some
fresh air, though. You look a bit pale and

pasty. Come on, let's go to the park. You've been hanging around inside for days."

"But I can't leave Ginger!" Amy cried at once. There was no way she'd be able to enjoy herself at the park while Ginger was poorly – she'd worry about him the whole time. "Please, Dad! Can't I stay here? I don't care about fresh air, I just want to look after Ginger."

Her dad hesitated. "Amy – kittens don't need looking after round the clock," he said gently. "Cats are very independent creatures. They don't mind being on their own."

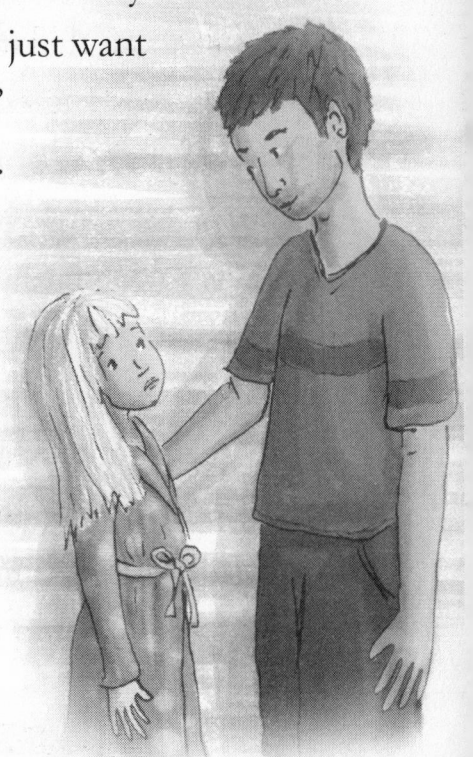

"But Ginger's only little," Amy pointed out. "And he's not well."

"I just think it might be good for you to get out, play with some other children…" her dad tried.

"I don't *know* any other children here," Amy said. "Ginger's my only friend now."

"What about the other girls with kittens?" her dad asked. "They seemed friendly. And we've got one of their phone numbers – Lily's, was it? Why don't I see if she wants to come round to play?"

Amy bit her lip. She *was* feeling kind of lonely, now that Dad mentioned it. But Lily was so bubbly and lively, she was probably the sort of girl who already had loads of friends. She was sure to be busy doing stuff with them – and it would be so embarrassing if Dad phoned, and Lily wasn't interested in seeing her. Amy's cheeks turned scarlet at the thought. "I don't think so," she said after a moment. "I'm fine with Ginger. Honestly."

"Well… If you're sure," her dad said, not sounding convinced. He sighed. "You know, Amy, we got you a kitten to help you settle in here. But we don't want having a kitten to mean you never go out and play!"

Amy shrugged. "I'm fine," she repeated. She couldn't think about playing or trying to make friends when Ginger was poorly. He was way more important, after all!

Chapter 6

On Saturday morning, Amy was supposed to have her first riding lesson, but Aunty Sarah phoned to cancel it, as some of the staff were ill. Amy didn't mind, it meant more time with Ginger! He seemed to be feeling much better, and was back to his playful self. Then, that afternoon, it was the first Kitten Club meeting. Amy had been looking forward to seeing the other girls and talking kittens with them, but now she was hit by an attack of nerves. Did the other girls *really* want her in the club? Maybe they had just felt sorry for her, Amy No-Mates, because she was new.

Her tummy felt fluttery as she walked up the path to Lily's front door, but Lily opened it with a smile. "Good, you're here," she said. "Come in, everyone's in the living room."

"See you later," Amy's mum called. "Have a great time!"

Amy followed Lily through to the living room, where the other four members of Kitten Club were sitting on the floor. Buster, Lily's black kitten, was running from one girl to the next, being petted and fussed over. He looked as if *he* was enjoying the first Kitten Club meeting already!

"Hey, Amy," Ruby said, as she walked in. "We were just talking about our code names. Have you thought of yours yet? I'm going to be Glamour-Puss!"

Amy smiled shyly. Ruby *was* a bit of a glamour-puss, it had to be said, with her painted fingernails and pretty earrings. "Perfect," she managed to say. "What are the rest of you called?"

"I was going to call myself KitKat, because I lurrrve chocolate," Molly said, "but with my name, I've got to be ... Moggy!"

Everyone laughed. "Hang on, let's write this down," Lily said. She opened up a big scrapbook and Amy saw that she'd already written "Kitten Club Meetings" in beautiful swirly handwriting at the top of the first page.

Lily lay down on her tummy and began writing the secret code names underneath.

Ruby ... Glamour-Puss

Molly ... Moggy

Lily ... Scatty

"S-cat-ty, get it?" she said with a grin. "Because I'm just a tiny bit forgetful. Anyone else? Ella, how about you?"

"My code name is going to be Tomboy," said Ella. "Because boy cats are called 'toms' and because everyone says I'm a bit of a tomboy." She wrinkled her nose. "I can't help it if I'm better at football and running than my twin brother though, can I?" She elbowed Mia. "What about you?"

"What? Oh!" said Mia. "I'll be … Witch-Cat!" she said, making a spooky face.

"That just leaves you, Amy. Have you got a code name?" Ruby asked.

Amy thought for a moment, and then her gaze settled on Buster, who had the most beautiful green eyes. Most cats had green eyes, didn't they? And so did Amy… "I'll be Green-Eyes," she said with a shy smile. She stroked Buster and picked him up. Goodness, he felt light as a feather compared to Ginger! *Amy … Green-Eyes,* wrote Lily, then put down her pen.

"Brilliant! So, Glamour-Puss, Moggy, Tomboy, Witch-Cat and Green-Eyes, welcome to Scatty's house," she said.

"Everyone who thinks Kitten Club is just the coolest club ever, say 'Meow'!"

"MEOW!" the girls chorused, and everyone giggled.

After they'd decided their code names, the six girls took it in turns to write a few sentences about their kittens in the scrapbook, and how they'd got along during their first week. Each of the kittens had such different personalities by the sound of things!

Smokey loves exploring, Mia wrote. *A bit too much! He's already managed to get shut in the laundry basket and in the cupboard under the sink! Luckily he's got such a loud meow I managed to track him down. He's an action kitten, all right — always up for an adventure!*

"Buster wouldn't know an adventure if it came and biffed him in the face," Lily said, tickling her kitten's tummy. "He's a right scaredy-cat, aren't you? He's been a bit lonely, I think. Mum says he hates it whenever I'm not here – he 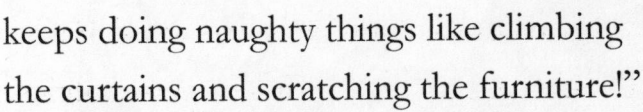 keeps doing naughty things like climbing the curtains and scratching the furniture!"

"Honey is a curtain-climber too," Ella said. "And she's been giving Misty – our other cat – a hard time. Poor Misty's an old lady cat, and she's not very keen on having Honey bouncing all over her!"

Amy wrote about Ginger and her swapping beds on the first night, which

made the others laugh, and then, once everyone had written something, they messed about on Lily's family's computer, designing certificates to say that they were official members of Kitten Club. Then they spent ages colouring them in. Amy decorated hers with a border of little paw-prints – it looked so cool!

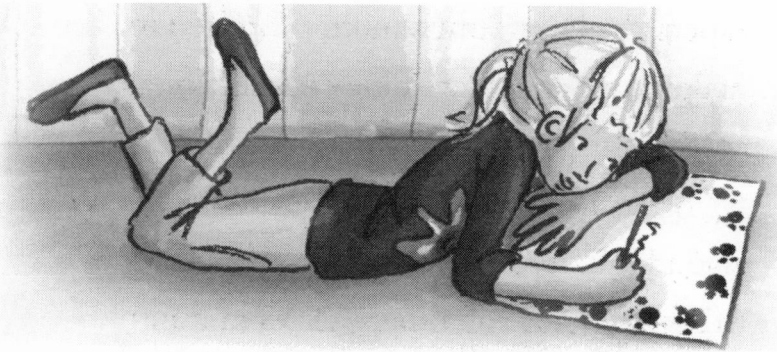

At four-thirty, the doorbell rang and everyone groaned. "Oh no!" Mia said. "It's not going-home time already, is it? I bet my mum's first, worst luck."

But it wasn't Mia's mum, it was Amy's. "Had a nice time, girls?" she asked, as she walked in.

"Yeah!" they all chorused.

She smiled. "Well, perhaps you could have the next Kitten Club meeting at Amy's house. What do you think?"

Everyone seemed to like that idea — especially when Amy's mum promised to make some chocolate-chip cookies for all of them!

Amy wrote down her phone number and address for everyone. "You're welcome to come round any time, girls," her mum said, as they were about to go. "We've only just moved to this area and don't know many people yet, so it would be great to see some friendly faces!"

"Cool," said Lily. "See you soon, then. Give Ginger a hug from me!"

As Amy said goodbye to her new friends and went off to the car with her certificate, she felt really happy. It was great to be part of Kitten Club – she couldn't wait for next Saturday!

Chapter 7

The following week slipped by just as quickly
as the first. Amy spent her time playing with
Ginger and looking after him. She'd bought a
bag of kitty treats at the pet shop and loved
making trails of them for him to find around
the house. Ginger liked that game too,
especially when he got to crunch up each
treat with his sharp little teeth!

Her mum and dad were still trying to persuade her to do things outside the house. Her mum had picked up a handful of leaflets about joining the Brownies, dance classes and swimming lessons, but Amy had stubbornly said no to all of them. She felt shy and nervous at the thought of having to meet lots of new people at once.

But then on Wednesday, an envelope addressed to Amy came through the post. The postmark was a local one and Amy ripped it open, wondering who had sent it. She pulled out a card which had a picture of two cats on the front. Inside, it said:

To Green-Eyes, can you come to tea at my house on Friday?
Love Glamour-Puss x
Tel: 01222 720 811

Amy felt really pleased. She really liked Ruby – or Glamour-Puss, rather! – and it would be nice to see Ruby's kitten Ziggy again. She got her dad to phone up immediately to say that yes, please, she'd love to go round for tea.

On Friday, before going to Ruby's house, Amy made a big fuss of Ginger. She brushed him carefully, then poured him a saucer of creamy milk. Just as she was pouring the milk, her dad called that it was time to go, making Amy jump and pour a bit more than she'd meant to. "Lucky for you, eh?" she said to Ginger, giving him a kiss goodbye.

She had a lovely time at Ruby's house. They played with Ziggy, made some

necklaces and bracelets from a bead set, and had fish-fingers and chips for tea. But when she got home later on, Amy was really upset to hear that poor Ginger had been sick on the kitchen floor again.

"Oh no!" she cried, rushing over to where he lay asleep in his cat bed. "Ginger, are you OK?"

"It might be because he had a different brand of kitten food today," her mum said. "We'll go back to the other sort, to see if that makes him feel better."

"OK," Amy said, but she still felt anxious. She hoped Ginger would be all right for Kitten Club the next day – she'd been looking forward to showing him off to everyone.

Luckily, Ginger seemed much better on Saturday morning, meowing loudly and trying to climb up Amy's chair as she sat eating her breakfast.

"Hmmm, is it me you love, or the smell of this bacon?" she asked, reaching down to stroke him. He immediately began trying to lick her fingers and she giggled. "Ooh, that tickles!"

She tried to carry on with her breakfast, but Ginger was now gazing up at her, mewing plaintively, his little nose twitching. Amy glanced at her parents. Her mum was buttering toast with her back turned, and her dad was looking in the fridge for ketchup.

"Go on, then," she whispered, unable to resist Ginger's begging any longer. She cut a

few small strips of bacon and dropped them under her chair, and he immediately gobbled them up. She smiled, pleased that Ginger was having a special Saturday breakfast too. It didn't seem fair that he should miss out!

Amy went to get dressed, but when she came downstairs twenty minutes later, her parents told her that Ginger had just been sick again. He lay in his cat bed, his eyes glassy and his body trembling.

Amy wanted to cry. She knelt down and stroked him, feeling churned up with worry. "Oh Mum," she said, biting her lip. "What's wrong with him? Do you think he's going to be all right?"

"He does seem to have a bit of a funny tummy," Mrs Wheeler replied. "If he's sick again, I think we'll have to take him to the vet's. Poor little thing. His tummy does look bloated." She glanced up at the clock. "Oh gosh, is that the time? We'll have to get you ready for your riding lesson soon."

Amy had forgotten all about her riding lesson. "Oh Mum, do I have to go?" she pleaded. "I won't be able to concentrate while Ginger's poorly. Please can't I stay here?"

"Well…" her mum replied.

"Please, Mum? I'll go next week, I promise!"

Amy's mum sighed. "All right. Just this once, then," she said. "I'd better phone Aunty Sarah and explain."

Ginger slept the whole morning under Amy's watchful eye and then, after lunch, it was time for the second Kitten Club meeting. She ran to the door as soon as she heard the bell. "Hiya," she said, feeling both excited and shy at the sight of Molly, Ruby and Lily on her doorstep. Then she smiled as she remembered their secret code names. "Hi, Moggy; hi, Glamour-Puss; hi, Scatty!"

"Yo, Green-Eyes," said Lily, putting on

an American accent and making everyone laugh. "Where's that cute little ginger powder-puff, then? I neeeeed to see him!"

"Ginger's in the kitchen," Amy said. "Come on through."

She led them into the kitchen where Ginger was still curled up fast asleep in the corner of his bed. "Awwww," Molly said quietly so as not to disturb him. "I love the way they wrap their tails around themselves, like a scarf. Truffle does just the same. It's so cute!"

Amy's mum came in to say hello. She poured glasses of lemonade and got out some cookies. "Help yourselves," she said. "I'll be in the garden if you need anything."

The doorbell chimed again and Amy went to let Mia and Ella in. "Are you OK?" Ella asked, kicking off her trainers in the hall. "I thought you might be at riding today."

"Ginger was sick and I didn't want to leave him," Amy explained. "He's all right now though. Come in. The others are here."

The girls sat down at the table, and Lily got out the club scrapbook. "Let's do the Kitten Club register," she said. "I'll call out your code name and…" Her eyes sparkled with merriment behind her glasses. "I know! When I say your name, you have to meow to say that you're here!"

The others laughed. "What are you like?" Molly said, shaking her head. "I feel as if I'm at school!"

"Moggy?" Lily asked, pen poised above the scrapbook.

"Meow, Miss Bossy-Boots," Molly replied.

"Green-Eyes?"

"Me— Oh! Ginger's awake!" Amy said, jumping up from her chair as she saw her kitten clambering out of his cat bed. "Perfect timing, Ginger. Are you feeling better?"

"Isn't he sweet? I love it when they're all sleepy," Ruby said, coming over to see him.

The other girls made their way over too. "Wow, hasn't he grown?" Mia said in surprise. "What a little porker!"

"Nothing *little* about him," Ella said. "Look at that belly! He's twice the size of Honey."

"He loves his food," Amy told them. "And his milk! He has a saucer of lovely creamy milk almost every day!"

Molly looked worried. "Kittens aren't supposed to have cows' milk," she told Amy.

"It's not good for their tummies. My mum said it can make them ill."

Amy felt her face turn hot. Oh dear. Was it the *milk* that had made Ginger sick? She bit her lip, feeling bad. His tummy did look very swollen still. "I gave him some bacon too," she confessed quietly, not able to look the others in the eye. "And … I suppose I have given him a lot of kitty treats lately…"

"No wonder he's so ginormous!" Lily blurted out. "Poor thing! You're not meant to feed kittens *that* much. He looks like he's about to explode!"

For a horrible moment Amy thought she was going to cry. "I was only trying to look after him!" she said defensively.

"I thought I was being kind!"

Ruby put an arm around her. "I know," she said. "But being kind to a kitten isn't all about dishing out treats."

"It's like being a parent," Mia put in. "I'm always asking for sweets, but my mum won't let me have them because they're so bad for my teeth." She shrugged, her dark eyes sympathetic. "I guess we have to be like that, too – even if our kittens seem to want something, we can't just give it to them every time."

A tear rolled down Amy's cheek. If only she'd listened to her aunt when she'd tried to talk to her about feeding Ginger. And there she'd been thinking what a brilliant kitten-mummy she was – when it was all her fault poor Ginger was sick!

Chapter 8

"Ginger will be all right," Molly said, stroking him gently. They were all sitting on the floor around him now. "Why don't you give him some water? If he's had bacon this morning, he might be thirsty. It always makes *me* feel thirsty when I eat it."

Amy got up and wiped away her tears with the back of her hand. Her fingers

trembled as she held Ginger's water bowl under the tap to fill it. How could she have been so stupid? She could have made Ginger really, really ill!

"Lucky for me and Ginger that I'm part of Kitten Club," she said shakily, as she put down the bowl. Ginger bent his head to it straight away and lapped up the water gratefully. "If it wasn't for you guys, Ginger might have ended up the size of a football!"

"Hey, we all make mistakes," Ruby said with a smile. She stroked Ginger's back and he started purring. "Ginger, my lad, you're going on a diet! But it's only because Amy loves you, OK?"

Ginger looked up from the water bowl, his head cocked and his eyes solemn as if he understood every word. *Meow*, he agreed.

The rest of the Kitten Club meeting was much happier. Amy even started to feel relieved now that she knew why Ginger had been poorly – at least it wasn't because there was something really badly wrong with him.

The girls wrote their kitten news in the scrapbook. Molly had had a panic when she couldn't find her kitten, Truffle, one day. "She gets so freaked out by the dog," Molly told the others, "and my big brothers, of course. I was looking for her for absolutely ages until I heard this little scared meow – and looked up to see her right on top of the

curtain rail! She'd managed to climb all the way up there – I couldn't believe it!"

"Poor Truffle," Mia said. "Smokey had an adventure too. I was out at gym club the other night, and I came back to find that my little sister Aisha had dressed Smokey in her doll's pyjamas – and tucked him up in her doll's cot!"

Everyone laughed. "I wish I could have seen that," said Ella. "Here, I've got some photos of Honey to stick in the book. Look – in this one, she's just about to pounce on Misty's tail!" She rolled her eyes. "Honey *loves* Misty – but the feeling is not mutual!"

After sharing their news, the girls drew some pet portraits to stick in the scrapbook, and then they all had a play with Ginger, who seemed a lot livelier again.

Once her friends had gone home, Amy went straight to her parents and admitted that she'd been secretly feeding Ginger too much, and spoiling him with milk, and that was why he'd been ill. "I just wanted to give him everything," she confessed. "He's all I've been thinking about…"

Her mum gave her a big hug. "I know," she said. "But perhaps you've doted on him a bit too much – at the expense of both of you! He needed less food, and you needed more time to do things for yourself, rather than constantly waiting on him."

"And maybe we're to blame, too," her dad put in, scooping up Ginger. "Perhaps we should have helped look after His Fluffy Highness more, not assume you could do everything yourself. And I should have made time to take you out more as well."

"I know it's hard, making a new start somewhere," her mum went on. "But you've got to be brave and just take the plunge sometimes. Luckily you've got the Kitten Club girls now – that's a good start. And do you know what else I found out today?"

"What?" Amy asked.

"I was talking to the mums while they were

waiting for your meeting to finish and I found out that Lily, Ruby and Mia are all starting at Brownies in the village…"

"Oh!" Amy said in surprise.

"And that Ella and her twin brother Finn have swimming lessons at the local leisure centre…"

"Cool!"

"And, best of all, that Molly and Ruby will be at your new school – so you'll get to see them there every day!" her mum finished. "What do you think of that?"

Amy felt as if the most massive weight had been lifted from her shoulders. She had been dreading starting school without knowing a single person there – so to find out that two members of Kitten Club would be with her was fantastic.

"That's brilliant news," she said happily. "Really, really brilliant!" She reached down to pick up Ginger, who was trying to climb up her leg. "I think it's going to be pretty good living here after all," she said, smiling. "And it's all down to you, Ginger. Without you, I wouldn't have met the Kitten Club girls. I'm so glad I did!"

Coming soon...

Sue Mongredien

Kitten Club

Smokey's Great Escape

To find out more about the author, visit:
www.suemongredien.co.uk